The Phone Call

Written by Susannah Reed

Illustrated by Stu McLellan

Collins

What's in this story?

Listen and say

lemonade

tie

Download the audio at www.collins.co.uk/839650

sandwich

bag

T-shirt

scissors

🎧 On Saturday morning, the phone rang in Ben's house.

"Who is calling?" thought Ben.

He ran down the stairs to the phone, but his mum answered it.

"Who is it?" asked Ben. "Is it for me?"

"No," said his Mum. "It's Jack's mum.
Their family would like to go for
a picnic today."

"Oh," said Ben.

The phone rang in Charlie's house.

Charlie ran to the kitchen, but his dad answered the phone.

"Is it for me?" asked Charlie.

"No," said his Dad. "It's Clare's dad. Clare is making lemonade for the picnic."

"Oh," said Charlie.

The families had a nice picnic. They ate sandwiches and they drank lemonade.

Then Ben's mum's phone rang.

"Is it for us?" asked Ben and Charlie.

"No, it isn't," said Ben's mum.

"Why are you asking?" asked Charlie's dad. "Who do you want to talk to?"

"You know, we did a competition!"
said Charlie.

NEW IDEAS
COMPETITION
DO YOU HAVE NEW IDEAS
FOR OLD THINGS?
WRITE TO US AT:

"A TV competition!" said Ben. "Look. They
wanted *new ideas for old things*."

"Wow, that's exciting!" said Jack.
"What's your idea?"

"Our idea is to make these bags from
old T-shirts," said Ben.

"Great!" said Clare. "How do you
make them?"

"You need an old T-shirt and some scissors," said Charlie.

top

bottom

"You cut the top and the bottom of the T-shirt," said Ben.

"You tie the bottom of the T-shirt and you make a bag." said Ben.

"That's clever!" said Jack.

"What a great idea!" said Clare.

"Look," said Charlie. "The people from the TV show *call everyone with the best ideas.*"
"Today!" said Ben.

"Hmm. Lots of people do competitions," said Ben's mum. "Not everyone wins."

"You're right," said Ben and Charlie. "Let's enjoy the picnic!"

Then Charlie's dad's phone rang.
Everyone stopped and looked at
the phone.

"Who's that?" asked Jack.

"I don't know," said Charlie's dad. "I don't
know the number."

"You answer it, Charlie," said Clare.

Charlie's dad gave the phone to Charlie.

"Hello?" said Charlie.

"Hello," said a woman. "I'm from the New Ideas competition. Can I talk to Ben Harper and Charlie Lucas, please?"

"This is Charlie Lucas," said Charlie.

"We loved your idea," said the woman.
"Can you come and talk about it
on Tuesday?"

"Yes, please!" said Charlie and Ben.

"Wow!" said Clare and Jack.

19

Clare went to Jack's house on Tuesday after school. They watched the New Ideas competition on TV.

Ben and Charlie talked about their bags. A different idea won the competition, but they were happy to be on TV.

"We can do this competition next time," said Jack.

"I have lots of ideas," said Clare.

"Me too!" said Jack.

"Ben and Charlie can help us," said Clare.

Picture dictionary

Listen and repeat

bag   lemonade   phone

picnic   sandwich   scissors

stairs   tie   top bottom

1 Look and order the story

2 Listen and say

Collins

Published by Collins
An imprint of HarperCollins*Publishers*
Westerhill Road
Bishopbriggs
Glasgow
G64 2QT

HarperCollins *Publishers*
Macken House,
39/40 Mayor Street Upper,
Dublin 1
D01 C9W8
Ireland

William Collins' dream of knowledge for all began with the publication of his first book in 1819.

A self-educated mill worker, he not only enriched millions of lives, but also founded a flourishing publishing house. Today, staying true to this spirit, Collins books are packed with inspiration, innovation and practical expertise. They place you at the centre of a world of possibility and give you exactly what you need to explore it.

10 9 8 7 6 5 4 3

ISBN 978-0-00-839650-3

Collins® and COBUILD® are registered trademarks of HarperCollins*Publishers* Limited

www.collins.co.uk/elt

British Library Cataloguing in Publication Data

A catalogue record for this publication is available from the British Library.

Author: Susannah Reed
Illustrator: Stu McLellan (Beehive)
Series editor: Rebecca Adlard
Commissioning editor: Zoë Clarke
Publishing manager: Lisa Todd
Product managers: Jennifer Hall and Caroline Green
In-house editor: Alma Puts Keren
Project manager: Emily Hooton
Editor: Frances Amrani
Proofreaders: Natalie Murray and Michael Lamb
Cover designer: Kevin Robbins
Typesetter: 2Hoots Publishing Services Ltd
Audio produced by id audio, London
Reading guide author: Emma Wilkinson
Production controller: Rachel Weaver
Printed and bound in the UK by Pureprint

MIX
Paper | Supporting responsible forestry
FSC™ C007454

This book is produced from independently certified FSC™ paper to ensure responsible forest management.

For more information visit:
www.harpercollins.co.uk/green

Download the audio for this book and a reading guide for parents and teachers at www.collins.co.uk/839650